JUN 1998

Celebrating
Mother's Day

By: Shelly Nielsen
Illustrated by: Marie-Claude Monchaux

Published by Abdo & Daughters, 4940 Viking Drive, Suite 622, Edina, Minnesota 55435.

Printed in the United States.

Illustrations by Marie-Claude Monchaux

Edited by Julie Berg

Library of Congress Cataloging-in-Publication Data

Nielsen, Shelly, 1958-
    Mothers Day / Shelly Nielsen.
        p. cm. -- (Holiday Celebrations)
    Summary: Rhyming text introduces aspects of this important day.
    ISBN 1-56239-704-4
    1. Mother's Day--Juvenile literature.[1.Mother's Day.]I. Title.
II. Series: Nielsen, Shelly, 1958-Holiday celebrations.
HQ759.2.N54 1996
394.2'68--dc20   96-12760
                                                      CIP
                                                      AC

Celebrating
Mother's Day

marie-claude monnaux

Jobs for Mom

Dear Mom,
Because it's Mother's Day
I did these special tasks—
walked the dog,
took out the trash,
(without being asked),
cleared the table,
helped wash the car,
and cleaned my cluttered room.
I didn't love the jobs,
but I sure love you!

My Mom is...

Our Mother's Day blackboard
says, "My Mom is..."
We have to finish the line,
every last kid.
I think and ponder
and search my mind.
Finally! I've got it!
"My Mom is...all mine!"

On Stage

Jenny first,
then Taylor,
then me...
We march single file
and join hands
to sing.

Mothers are what
our program's about.
Breathe deep.
Ready?
Sing out!

Love Note

"I LOVE YOU, MOM,"
I carefully wrote.
Now...
where to hide my secret note?
I know!
Under her pillow
with a ribbon tied 'round...
I can't wait for my note
to be found.

Dinner Out

Dad and I took Mom to dinner
as a special treat.
We held her chair out for her,
and said, "Have anything to eat."
Our manners were the finest,
we made such a big fuss;
if Mom hadn't known us both so well,
she'd have never guessed it was us.

Picture This

I like to look at photographs
from a long time ago.
Mom looks different,
all dressed in funny clothes.
In this picture, I'm a baby,
and Mom's holding me up.
We've changed so much
since way back then
we hardly recognize us!

To my Mother

marie claude monchaux

Photo Frame

We made these cards at school today.
Outside I wrote, "To My Mother."
My photo is taped to one side
and Mom's is on the other.

Cards! Cards! Cards!

Mother's Day cards,
Mother's Day cards,
A million...
A trillion...
Cards by the yards!
Every store packed
with cards to the ceiling,
full of flowers
and gushy feelings.
I like the pictures,
colors and lace,
but no card is as good
as the one that I made.

Kisses, Kisses

These X's cut from paper
are only good for this—
hand one to me anytime
and you will get a kiss.

Paper Bouquets

Cut paper petals
in yellow, pink, and blue,
then carefully
push a wire through.
Gather your flowers and
add a satin bow.
Give them to your mother;
they'll surprise her so!

Homework

"What reminds you most of Mom?
Bring something to school."
That's what our teacher
asked us to do.
Mandy brought running shoes
(her mom jogs).
John showed a picture of a bus
(driving is his Mom's job).
But I brought the blanket
that's spread upon my bed
because each night Mom tucks me in
and kisses my head.

Breakfast Surprise

I toasted bread,
peeled an orange,
and put everything on a tray.
Ready? *Shh!*
I tiptoed up the stairs,
What would Mama say?
Knock, knock, knock.
"Happy Mother's Day,"
I quietly said.
Mama couldn't believe her eyes:
breakfast in bed!